This book is dedicated to granddaughters
Daphne, Zoe, Emma, Olivia
Grandnieces June, Cassidy, Marley,
Josey, Kyla, Rosie, Mira,
Grandnephews Cooper, Chase, Vaughn, Asa, Levi,
Omar, Cole, Wyatt, Eddie and Cormac
Their very existence pushed me to finish this project
before they were too old to appreciate it.

Thank you to my wife, Joanne, for her love
and support, to my sister, Loretta, poet laureate
of the family for her editorial insights and to
Sarah Pruitt for her artwork.

Lastly, a special thanks to my nephew, Aaron,
who in his short life showed me
that one must find your gifts,
trust your heart, be open to others and dare,
for the world is yours to discover.

Ever Wish?

by Larry Lindberg

Illustrations by Ayin Visitacion

with artistic input from Sarah Pruitt

The characters were created

by the author

but brought to life

by Jessie Fox Nystrom

Begin your adventure with us!

Ever wish...
to be a bird
in the air,
a lion, a tiger
or huge grizzly bear?
How about an elk
so proud and so tall
or a mouse on the floor
so meek and so small?
Think of a fish
in a stream
or a duck on a lake,
a lizard, an elephant
or even a snake.

So hard to choose?
Can't you decide?
Here's an idea
for you to try.
Why pick just one
when you can pick two?
You can put them together,
slightly askew.
You'll now have a friend
that's quite unique.
It's yours all alone
whether it roars
or it squeaks.

Think up anything.
Don't worry,
it's totally free.
An alligator-fly
or goat-squid in
the sea,
a dog-like canary
or a fish bumblebee.
Look, weasel-frogs
croaking and
jumping with glee.
Some examples in
nature you've
probably heard,
like the big
tiger-shark
or the small cowbird.

What about a
catfish,
dogfish and
parrotfish too,
or the whale shark
too big for the zoo?
Ever see a horse fly?
Funny, I can.
Pegasus from
mythology,
what a wing span!
Not real? That's the
point, don't you see?
So, let's give it
a try.
What shall it be?
Wait, let me go first-

Turn the page and
you'll see...

The Hippopiper is a bird
as far as I can tell,
but it's not born like you or me
only hatched from a shell.
Their bodies are big and round
atop long skinny stems,
and on their feet, sharp little nails,
buffed and polished as gems.
The feathers on this amazing bird
are large and quite small,
arranged below its waist and neck
where it has no feathers at all.
These Pipers are so tall
when they're standing erect,
if you hope to see their face,
you likely will strain your neck.

They would be more
friendly, you see,
if they weren't
in such pain,
but with a body
this size,
its feet can't
stand the strain.
A Piper
doesn't travel much
as some birds
of this type and kind,
so it stays close
to a rocky nest
which it doesn't
seem to mind.

They don't peck like
smaller birds
because their beaks
are blunt.
They only eat from
the mud such things
they do not
have to hunt.
These birds, in fact,
don't run or jump
and of course
they cannot fly.
If they could,
you'd have to watch out
or be hit by a
Hippopiper PIE!

Here's a long neck giant.
The Eleraffe is quite a fellow.
He has a long trunk-like nose
and fur spotted brown and yellow.
Being biggest of all the beasts
you'd think he'd be too rough,
but we have a baby here now
so care is not that tough.
We have a large yard and fence
and he's happy staying here.
We feed him lots of leaves and hay
so the trees don't have to fear.
He drinks a lot with his longish trunk,
but needs to bend his neck,
finishing off our garden pond
without ever getting wet.

Eleraffes can't
run very fast
or leap or
jump a fence,
but they can step
over most of that
so jumping
makes no sense.
I like to take
him for walks
when he needs a
chance to roam.
The neighborhood
is not the same
until I bring
him home.

He enjoys us
on his back
or climbing
his legs and tail,
but what he likes
best is to
wash him off
with a hose,
a mop and a pail.
When he grows
to his full size,
we'll keep him
on our farm.
He'll have lots
of friends and
space and
nothing to
do him harm.

Bumble Bats have a sound
when they fly right by,
reminding me of airplanes
high up in the sky.
They at first appear a bee,
but grow to such a size,
with a face more like a dog
their looks are a surprise.
To keep one as a pet is great,
but better have four or five.
B-Bats like to hang in a group
and make a kind of hive.
With bodies all black and yellow,
plus being so very hairy,
when they all fly together
it can be pretty scary.

B-Bats stay
busy as other bees
and love to
fly at night.
Though they flutter
around like moths,
they really don't
like the light.
Pollination is
their thing,
finding the
biggest flowers.
But they also
catch flying bugs,
often eating them
for hours.

Bumble Bats are
full of joy
when they get
out and fly.
Keeping them
happy in a cage
requires a special
kind of pie.
It's made with
berries and nuts,
with a bunch
of snails and slugs.
Last goes in
their favorite treat.
You guessed it,
fat little bugs.

Cowcadiles are really cool
since they give milk and eggs.
It's very hard to get the milk
because they have short legs.
They do kind of fight and bite
with huge teeth and jaws,
and on their large three-toed feet
are long and curved sharp claws.
When you want them to behave
like other kinds of cows,
gently raise their tail up high
and they will obey the laws.
Cowcadiles have few friends
of mammal or reptile bent,
but when they slide into the water,
the fish are first to consent.

They all dive and
splash and swim
and really act
like friends.
But these fish
just steal milk
and never
make amends.
You see Cowcas
now and then
out in a
swamp or bog,
just hanging
out in herds
or all alone
on a log.

They are the
kind of pet
that's very
hard to keep,
unless there's
a swimming pool
with a fence
they cannot leap.
Of course, if
they're well fed
Cowcas are like
a Teddy,
but we had one
who missed a meal
and he bit our
old dog Freddie.

Kangorillas, though seldom seen,
can hop and hang and box.
They love to play with ropes and sticks
and wear colorful pairs of socks.
Having a pouch like 'roos or Koalas
they hardly ever use it,
except for keeping a fruit inside
in case someone might bruise it.
The color of their fur is strange
as it changes by and by
from reddish brown to purplish green
to hide them when they're shy.
You'd expect them to be very large
with monster legs and back,
but that's not the case with them
because size is what they lack.

The typical K-Gor
as they're called
are sort of
short and stout,
with long hair
around their neck
and all along
their snout.
I do love him
so very much as
we romp or
read a book,
but try not to be
too rough,
he has a powerful
right hook.

He knocked me down
on my seat,
boxing with him
one night.
So now when
things get rough
and I want to
prevent a fight,
I hug the little
furry fellow
which greatly
calms him down.
Then we share a mango
from his pouch
and watch the
sun set over town.

Now it's your turn!

Start with
a thought
or a name
in your head.
Something that
came to you
lying in bed
or walking along
with a friend
or a pet.
Let it pop out!
It's there,
you can bet.

Now draw
a tail
or a hoof
or an ear,
and then
a face
with a grin
or a sneer.
Add lots
of teeth
or a long skinny
tongue.
Give it big
hairy feet.
Make it old,
make it young.

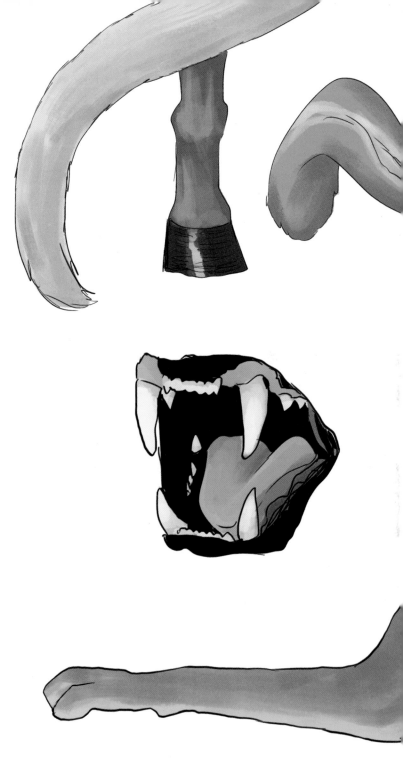

Can't you think
of a thing?
Well, here's a list
of a few
of my friends
with some funny
little twists.
How about Weasel-frogs?
Please do make
a note.
There's a
humpback
Buffalizard
or an Owligoat...

Rhinostriches
or those
Gatorbats.
How about
Eleanteaters
or Platapussycats?
There is a beautiful
Tigeraffe or a
Mongooseduck.
Have you seen a
Ram-nah-saurus,
big as a truck?

Now, here you go,
so let's get to it!
See what's in there,
you certainly can do it!

Author's Note

Do you think Jessie Fox and I are crazy for coming up with these mixed-up creatures? Would you believe truth is stranger than fiction? For a hundred or more years, the following animals have existed for real. Some were created by people, others happened in nature due to climate change or loss of habitat.

We've all heard of Mules (horse-donkey). What about the Liger (lion-tiger), a very popular creation found in Japan, France and the USA? It is the world's largest cat at nearly six feet tall and weighing a thousand pounds.

The list of strange animal combinations is long. Felines (cats) include Tigon (tiger-male and lion-female), Jaglion (jaguar-lion), Leopon (leopard-lion) and Savannah cat (African Wild-Siamese). Canines, like wolves and dogs, include the Coydogs (coyote-dog), Coywolf or Woyote (coyote-wolf). With bears, we've only one so far, the Grolar bear (grizzly-polar) which happened in nature and captivity. Some other species we found were the Zonkey (zebra-donkey) and the Zorse (zebra-horse).

Mules (horse-donkey) have been around for many centuries and used to ride, pack goods or even pull a plow. Goldfinch-Canary offspring are also called mules.

There are the Cama (camel-llama), Yakon (yak-cow), Cattalo (cattle-buffalo), Geep (goat-sheep) and the Iron Age pig (wild boar-pig). In the Oceans we have the Wholphin (orca-bottle-nosed dolphin) and Narluga (beluga whale-narwhals).

Killer bees are a combination of African bees and European Honey bees. They were created in a lab in Brazil in 1956 to increase honey production. The test failed and in 1957 numerous hives escaped into the wild. These Africanized bees are now found across the southern US from California to Georgia.

Finally, there was a special tri-animal creation around 1905 in Chicago where a litter of Lijanleps was born to a lion male and a Jagulep (jaguar-leopard) female. Several more litters were born over time and were shown in exhibitions as Congolese Spotted Lions.

Is all this experimentation wrong? I'm not sure, but it certainly is an imaginative test of our natural world.

A note about Freddie the dog: Although he gets bitten in my poem, Freddie lived a long life as my wife's trusted friend. His loyalty, intensity and agility (considering he had only three legs) are legendary. How he lost his leg and the rest of his story are being reserved for another book.

Jessie Fox is a Portland artist who loves to incorporate humor in her work. She started her business, Whatif Creations, in 2013 based on an illustration series involving hybrid animals and wordplay. The idea began while she was working at a residential treatment facility for troubled youth.

Portland, OR

After discovering their fondness for humorous art, she was able to build rapport with her caseload by drawing for them. Jessie's Whatif creatures have evolved into a series of playful, smart, contemporary products that can be found at Portland Saturday Market or online at www.whatifcreations.com.

To order additional copies of this book, contact:
Xlibris
1-888-795-4274
www.Xlibris.com
Orders@Xlibris.com

ISBN: Softcover   978-1-7960-7225-9
           Hardcover   978-1-7960-7224-2
           EBook   978-1-7960-7223-5

Printed in the United States of America

Rev. date: 02/27/2020